SHUSH H

(CONVERSATIONS WITH MY CAT)

BOB CARRINGTON

ILLUSTRATED BY TRACIE CLARKE-PIGGOT

DEDICATIONS

Mum and Dad - They wouldn't have got it but would have definitely understood.

My baby sister Susan and brother-in-law Matt, vassals to their own tribe of cats.

Hettie - bestie. Mother to the mad bonkers Charlie, a loony Springer Spaniel who has a liking for eating remotes and now changes channels by barking at the TV set. Both cared for by Lady Bella and Princess Willow.

The previous Lords and Ladies who have so graciously shared their lives with me - Ragnar, Freya, Loki, Nix, Salem, Spook, Katie & Charlie, Fluffy, Willie Wombat, And the feller who started it all, Scran. Also, a mention to Rebel, who wasn't a cat, but I'm sure would have been made an honorary member of the feline fraternity.

If I've forgotten anyone, it's because I'm old and my memory is going, and I most respectfully apologise. I hope Cat Valhalla is treating you all well.

Acknowledgements

Glynn James, a "real" author, his stuff is all made up (though I'm convinced he believes it's all true and he's merely reporting actual events). His guidance, assistance, technical know-how, real time practical input, and company in the pub on a weekday afternoon, went a long way to making this possible. Check out his books on Amazon and may the impending apocalypse continue to inspire him.

Tracie Clarke-Piggot for her brilliant illustrations and Pub Landladyness.

The Little Ale House, Wellingborough for the small matter of BEER! "Hello me duck".

Debbie, Keiron, Lewis, Lucy, Jax - It's your fault.

All my CWMC Facebook followers, who actually gave me some encouragement to take this further. You may yet regret it.

Search for **Shush hooman - Conversations with my Cat** on Facebook. A link will appear on my personal page if it's not there already.

And, of course, the Majestic Lady Lagertha, the star of the whole thingymajig, without whose permission to commence and approval of the finished article, I could not have attempted the project.

FOREWORD

The Norse Goddess Freya (or Freyja) in her Chariot pulled by pussy cats.

During the night of the late August Bank Holiday 2022, my lovely boy, Ragnar, died (I hate the term "passed away"). He'd gotten ill very quickly, and I was actually planning on trying to find a vet's who may have been open on the Bank Holiday Monday. As it happened, I found him in the neighbour's garden in the morning. I hope his spirit made it to the cat equivalent of Valhalla.

At that point I was probably not looking to share my house and life with another cat. I'm knocking on a bit, and they can be a bit of a handful. Not long after I was in the pub and a friend called Debbie spoke to me about a couple she knew who were looking for a new home for a young cat they had and was I interested. I didn't know to be honest, though it seemed a good fit. A few days later Debbie sent me a picture and I was lost. Arrangements were made and she came to me about a week later. She wasn't known as Lagertha at that time by the way but didn't seem to mind the change. The rest is history.

Everything in this book actually happened. There may be inaccuracies in the translation from Cat to Hooman, although the flavour of the conversations is spot on. The difficulties in translation arise from the fact that Cats speak in a hybrid language consisting partly of Egyptian Hieroglyphics, that as everyone knows, is a visual, pictorial language only. Hence the translation difficulties.

All errors are mine (I've been told to add that bit).

FANCY A CHAT?

Me: So why have you dragged the food off the saucer on to the floor?

Cat: Cats are sensitive to their hooman vassal's needs. Eating off the floor will save the hooman washing the saucer.

Me: But the saucer already needed washing, now I have to clean the floor as well.

Cat:

Me: Um.

Cat:

Me: So...

Cat: Cats are superior beings, hoomans should accept decisions that are in their best interests.

Me: But..

Cat: Shush hooman.

ONE CAT'S ART IS ANOTHER MAN'S DISASTER

Me: So, can we talk about the wallpaper?

Cat: Um, wallpaper?

Me: Yes. The little scraps of wallpaper all down the stairs.

Cat: Oh, you mean the excess waste from my Immersive Art Installation. Didn't want to seem Anti-Eco so turned it into a trail.

Me: Huh?

Cat: You haven't seen it. Go take a look.

THIRTY SECONDS LATER

Me: But that's, that's......

Cat: Yes, I know, good innit?

Me: But it's supposed to stay on the wall.

Cat: You just don't appreciate Feline Art.

Me: But.......

Cat: Shush hooman.

I AM INNOCENT

Me: So, can I ask you about the cat food pouches all over the kitchen floor?

Cat: Sorry, me no understand.

Me: The food you eat. It comes in pouches that come in boxes.

Cat: Yes, and...

Me: Well one of the opened boxes looks like it's been attacked by someone with claws and 2 pouches on the floor are leaking from small claw shaped punctures.

Cat: So, you're blaming me.

Me: Well, you're the only clawed being in my house.

Cat: Your house???? We'll come back to that issue. Anyway, you got pictures? You always have pictures.

Me: No, obviously it happened overnight.

Cat: Hah. Typical, blame the poor defenceless cat.

Me: Look.....

Cat: Shush hooman.

ANYONE GOT A SILVER BULLET?

Me: So, busy night then?

Cat: Huh! What?

Me: Well, the bag of cat litter looks like it's been attacked by a werewolf....... or a cat.

Cat: Probably the werewolf then. Anything else?

Me: Curtains at the front window. Little rips seem to have appeared and the curtain rod is slightly bent, almost as if a......

Cat: ..... a werewolf was trying to climb them. Totally got ya.

Me: I heard scratching and ripping noises early morning, all I saw was a dark blob streaking away. Turned the light on and 2 prints are hanging off the wall in shreds.

Cat: Like ninjas them werewolves.

Me: And finally, the cat vomit in the middle of the living room floor.

Cat:

Me: Well?

Cat: Yep, that was me.

Me: Wait. You're admitting it?

Cat: Sure. Did you clean it up?

Me: Yes, but....

Cat: Cool (yawn), think I'll have a nap.

Me: But....

Cat: Shush hooman.

"I believe cats to be spirits come to earth. A cat, I am sure, could walk on a cloud without coming through." – Jules Verne

CAT FCAT

Cats first lived in Ancient Egypt. This came about because in the really olden times, all the different Gods had a meeting to divvy up the World (and the Universe as it happens, but that bit came after lunch). When it came to the agenda item about Cats, there wasn't a lot of enthusiasm to make a decision. Eventually, after a lot of pointless faffing, Father Odin made a statement and the minutes show that this is what he said.

"Well, lacking any other suggestions, why don't we put them in Ancient Egypt? The place is like a giant litter tray anyway".

So, this is what happened. It later came to light that Osiris, who's turn it was to represent the Ancient Egyptian Pantheon at that particular meeting, was actually asleep so missed the whole debate, otherwise things could have been very different.

"In ancient times cats were worshipped as gods; they have not forgotten this."
– Terry Pratchett

FAIL, FAIL, ROCK N' ROLL

Me: Um, can I ask you about the radio?

Cat: Sorry, the what?

Me: Radio. The thing that plays the music in the mornings when I wake up.

Cat:

Me: You know. On the drawers near my bed.

Cat: Oh, you mean that boxy thing that makes that infernal noise while I'm trying to nap?

Me: Uh-huh. Anyway, I stretched out my arm this morning and it wasn't there.

Cat: What? Your arm wasn't there.

Me: No, the radio wasn't there. It was on the floor. Did you push it off.

Cat:

Me: Well?

Cat: Nope. Definitely wasn't me. Now before you start, I know I do push small things off tables and stuff, but I know you love that noise maky thing, so I wouldn't.

Me: Hmm. Could it have been accidental when you did one of your night-time explorations?

Cat: No, no, no. Maybe the werewolf.

Me: (sigh) there is no wer.... Anyway, fortunately it still works.

Cat: Damn!

Me: What?

Cat: I mean GREEEEEAAAT.

Me: So, do you think you could maybe, be more careful?

Cat: Nap time. Shush hooman.

"Cats choose us; we don't own them." – Kristin Cast

SOCK IT TO ME

Me: Morning, can we talk about the clothes airer?

Cat: Sure, wait, the whattity what?

Me: The clothes airer, the wooden thing I sometimes put up in the bathroom to dry my clothes.

Cat: Ah! You mean my climbing frame. Don't know where it came from, but it's really cool. Anyway, your point.

Me: Well two things. My damp socks and underwear seem to be scattered all over the bathroom floor with bits of cat hair stuck to them and...

Cat: Probably werewolf hair, anyhow what else?

Me: There is no were.... God help me. Also, one of the struts seems to be broken.

Cat: Ah no, that's not damage, that's a modification.

Me: Huh?

Cat: Just to make it harder.

Me: But....

Cat: Anyway, please don't put wet things on my climbing frame.

Me: It's not a...

Cat: Shush hooman.

LATE NIGHT EMERGENCY

Me: So, did you have an emergency charge downstairs early this morning?

Cat: Sorry, what?

Me: Around 2ish I think. I heard you fly out the spare bedroom and run down the stairs.

Cat: Nope wasn't me.

Me: But look at this photo of your litter tray. It all looks a bit frantic and desperate. I also heard some manic scrabbling.

Cat: Nope, deffo not me, maybe another cat.

Me: There is no other cat.

Cat: The werewolf then.

Me: Oh dear. There are no were.....

Cat: Shush hooman.

SNUG AS A BUG

Cat: So, do you like my new house?

Me: It's a rug.

Cat: No, it's definitely a house.

Me: It's a rug that you've somehow managed to fold in half.

Cat: Nope. House.

Me: It's also a rug that you've somehow managed to fold in half that I need to move so that I can leave the room.

Cat: Stuck here with me then. You're not coming into my house though.

Me: I need to leave the room to replenish stores of food. Your food too.

Cat:

Me: Well?

Cat:

Me: So wha......

Cat: Shush hooman.

CAT ON THE CHEST

Me: Good Morning young lady. You haven't done this for a while.

Cat: Feline Goddesses sometimes deem their hoomans worthy of attention.

Me: Your food bowl is empty, isn't it?

Cat: Yes.

Me: Just a few more min.....

Cat: Shush hooman..... and get up.

CAT HACK

Me: Um, Internet isn't working too well.

Cat: I have no idea what you're talking about.

Me: The Internet. You know that small, white box near the curtains.

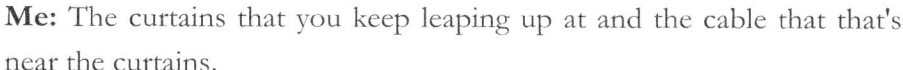

Cat: Umm......

Me: The curtains that you keep leaping up at and the cable that that's near the curtains.

Cat: Err....

Me: It looks like the cable has been pulled and the tab on the little white box is bent.

Cat: And why is this relevant to me.

Me: Well, it's affecting the Internet connection and so hampering my efforts to resupply your food.

Cat:

Me: Any thoughts?

Cat: Buy a new one. And get some food at same time.

Me: I think you're missing the point.

Cat: Shush hooman and get your shopping bag.

"Dogs come when they're called; cats take a message and get back to you later." — Professor Mary Bly

CAT FCAT

It seems that Father Odin later regretted plonking the Cats in Ancient Egypt and later, though still in olden times, showed some real affection for them. This was reinforced by the Goddess Freya, who, for no apparent reason, took a fancy to the idea of having her chariot pulled by cats and so had a quick word in the boss's ear.

Father Odin then sent a message to the Cats in Ancient Egypt suggesting an alternative homeland. This was met with approval by some of the Cats but not all of them. The more hairy ones quite fancied a break from the stifling heat of the desert, but the smoother skinned ones were quite happy soaking up the rays and the grounds were set for what was to become known as "The Great Cat Split".

LOOKS LIKE ITS CURTAINS

Cat: Can I have some food then?

Me: Just a mo, let me finish putting this stuff on my shoulder.

Cat: Smells a bit odd. Not food, is it?

Me: No, it's not food. It's to help with a bit of pain.

Cat: Hurty stuff. How did that happen?

Me: Well Saturday night when you jumped from the table up onto the curtains....

Cat: Ah! You grabbed me. Didn't like that much. Although you were a bit quick. Not like Feline Speed but not bad.

Me: Thanks, anyw......

Cat: Why'd you grab me?

Me: You can't be on the curtains; you might pull them down. Please don't do it again.

Cat: mumble, mumble, mumble.

Me: Sorry, what?

Cat: Nothing. So, you're in pain?

Me: It's not too bad actually but....

Cat: So, you're okay to feed me?

Me: Well, if you could just....

Cat: Like now.

Me: But...

Cat: Now.

Me: If....

Cat: Shush hooman. Food.

"You know how it is with cats: They don't really have owners, they have staff." — Author PC Cast

SINKING FEELING

Me: Morning, you doing the washing up?

Cat: Hooman. Curb your insolence. Menial tasks are not for Cats, that is why I have you.

Me: Umm. Okay, so why are you sitting on the sink?

Cat: Obviously, I am having a drink of water.

Me: But you have water, near the door.

Cat: Hooman. You clearly have no concept of true Felineness. Are you seriously suggesting that drinking out of a bland, white, plastic bowl is more exciting than capturing water drops out of this strange, alien tentacle thing.

Me: You're drinking out of the tap (sigh!).

Cat: You make it sound so boring.

Me: Anyway, can you jump down? I need to do the washing up as you're not going to.

Cat: Shush hooman. I'm having fun.

Me: But....

Cat: Shush.

POKKY LIPS NOW

Me: Hi there. Umm, you okay?

Cat: Yesss. Why?

Me: Err, couple of nights ago I heard you scrabbling around on the......

Cat: Scrabbling!!! Exploring and Investigating I think you'll find.

Me: Right, okay. Well, I heard an initial clunk that sounded like something hitting the floor and then sounds of lots of charging around the room and additional clunky noises.

Cat: Huh uh.

Me: Well, this morning I noticed a small penknife missing off the shelf. I can't find it anywhere.

Cat: (sigh) Your point.

Me: So, you must have knocked it off and played with it and err......

Cat: Oh, you mean the shiny, heavy thing. No, it was trying to escape.

Me: Escape? It has no life, it's an inanimate object, it can't.....

Cat: I saw it keep creeping towards the edge. I tried to catch it and then I was chasing it around the room to return it to its proper place.

Me: FFS. Well okay, where is it now?

Cat: Hiding I should think.

Me: Hiding! It's a penknife. It has no sentience.

Cat: Anyway. I hear you always going on about the impending Pokky Lips.

Me: Huh! Pokky Lips........ oh, you mean Apocalypse.

Cat: Always handy to have some protection around....... assuming I can find it.

Me: Holy f....

Cat: Also useful in Werewolf attacks.

Me: There are no freaking were.....

Cat: Shush hooman. Food time.

DUVET DAY

Cat: What's up hooman?

Me: I'd just like to thank you for helping me change the bedding the other day.

Cat: Absolute pleasure.

Me: Although it turned a ten-minute job into over half an hour.

Cat: Shouldn't rush things. Taking your time means a job well done.

Me: You know that sneaking under the fitted sheet makes it hard to pull the other corners in.

Cat: Security check. Making sure no one, or werewolves, had infiltrated.

Me: And crawling into the duvet cover several times, makes it harder for me to fit....

Cat: I was pulling from the other end, making sure the corners fit nicely.

Me: I'm also baffled how you found the entrance to the pillowcase as it was folded up.

Cat: Magic.

Me: Hard to squeeze a pillow in when it's full of cat.

Cat: We got there in the end did we not?

Me: We? Never mind. I'm curious why on previous occasions you've just sat and watched without interfering and...

Cat: Interfering?

Me: Err, helping. Anyway, why this time.

Cat: Got to figure it out first, innit?

Me: (sigh) I suppose it's food time?

Cat: Shu... well done hooman, training is coming along.

Me: Than.....

Cat: Shush.

FRUIT FROLLICS

Cat: Morning hooman. You don't mind me snuggling under the blanket, do you? I can move if you like.

Me: Uh, morning, no that's fine, wait, why are you being polite?

Cat: I just want to say sorry about the tomatoes.

Me: Tomatoes? Why, what's happened?

Cat: They seem to be all over the kitchen floor and the little box they live in is upside down.

Me: What? How? Did you....?

Cat: Wasn't me. I'm guessing they were depressed with suicidal tendencies and threw themselves off the unit.

Me: What?

Cat: I don't think the satsumas had the same problem though.

Me: Satsumas? I'm confused.

Cat: They're on the kitchen floor also.

Me: Oh FFS. How did th......

Cat: Pretty sure you don't have suicidal satsumas though. Looks like that nice gothic goblet knocked them off.

Me: Whaaaat?

Cat: Yep. That's on the floor too. Don't look at me like that, I'm as upset as you, a bit. I feel for you really.

Me: Bloody hell, I'd better get up then.

Cat: Good idea. You could maybe feed me when you get to kitchen, err before you sort out the tomatoes and satsumas, then I can get out of your way.

Me: It definitely wasn't you????

Cat: Oh please. Shush hooman.

BIT OF A RUCK

Me: Hallo. You comfy?

Cat: Yes thanks.

Me: I notice that you're lying on my backpack.

Cat: Yep. That's okay, isn't it? I mean us cats are okay with cold, hard floors but a wee bit of comfort is always appreciated.

Me: Sure, err I guess that's not really a problem but, umm, how the backpack got onto the floor is.

Cat: Uh huh.

Me: I mean it was hanging on the wall so I'm guessing you jumped up and hung off one the straps.

Cat: Sounds about right. What's the actual issue?

Me: Well, you didn't actually unhook it.

Cat: We are awesome as a species but it's a bit tricky to unhook things while hanging from front paws and not having thumbs.

Me: Sure, but the hook is also on the floor.

Cat:

Me: With a bit of the wall still attached to it.

Cat:

Me: So I......

Cat: Small bit though.

Me: Yes but....

Cat: I mean, really small.

Me: I know but....

Cat: Shush hooman, food.

HAMMER HORROR?

Me: So, err, bit of a wild night then?

Cat: When?

Me: Well last night obviously.

Cat: Sorry, confused. I was asleep most of it.

Me: What about the bit when you weren't asleep?

Cat: On security patrol I'd imagine. What exactly is the problem?

Me: The trail of destruction downstairs.

Cat: Ah! I did think I heard growling at one point. Maybe the werewolf is back.

Me:

Cat: Do you think?

Me:

Cat: Hooman, are you okay?

Me: I'm just going to lie down.

Cat: Can you just refresh my food first?

Me: (Groan!).

Cat: Shush hooman.

CAT FCAT

Around about the time that Howard Carter was rummaging around amongst Tutankhamen's remains, and so bringing all manner of deathly curses (not cat related by the way) down upon his mates, another equally important, but less publicised discovery was made over at the Sphinx.

Following a sandstorm, a worker who had snuck round the back for a quick smoke, noticed what he thought was ancient writing near the base of the construction. Experts were summoned, but not from Howard Carter's party as things were not going well amongst that group. These experts quickly established that it was not ancient writing, but scratch marks.

Further excavation revealed a hinged, stone flap. This was quickly widened, and the experts found their way into a previously undiscovered chamber containing shelves of scrolls and ornaments. Curiously a few of these ornaments were lying in pieces on the floor. An inspection of the track marks in the dust suggested that these ornaments had at some point been pushed off the shelving. Furthermore, some of the scrolls were flattened and torn.

However, one piece of damaged scroll had some legible writing on it, unfortunately the damaged parts had apparently shown the name of an unknown feline so we cannot say who it was.

However, the wording was eventually translated and says.

"Blimey it's hot around here, I'm heading North, anyone coming?"

AAAAAH

Cat: Morning hooman, are you well?

Me: Yes, I am, how about you?

Cat: I'm good. Just like to say how nice it was to let me snuggle up under the duvet with you last night. All warm and cosy.

Me: You're right. It was nice.

Cat: Thanks, hooman.

Me: My absolute pleasure.

CATNAP

Me: Hey, what's with the scratching?

Cat: Well, you're trying to get in my bed.

Me: Your bed, this is my bed. I've just been to the loo.

Cat: We've swapped. You can have one of my beds downstairs.

Me: You mean one of those boxes that you can hardly fit in?

Cat: Err yeah. They're really cosy.

Me: No, they're not. Might be for cats but....

Cat: Look, just put the duvet back over me and toddle off.

Me: Well, consider this. If I can't get into MY bed, I may get ill because of the cold and die. This will lead to lack of food. For cats.

Cat:

Me: So?

Cat: Hmm. I hear dead hoomans can be quite tasty in an emergency.

Me: Oh please.

Cat: Okay get in. No rolling over and no windypops.

Me: Thank you very....

Cat: Shush hooman. Pull the duvet over and go to sleep.

KEEP SHARP THING AWAY FROM HOOMANS

Me: Um, busy night then?

Cat: Sorry, what?

Me: Well, I found my nail scissors in the bathroom, they were on the dressing table.

Cat: Nail scissors??

Me: Never mind. Just be careful as they can open and hurt you.

Cat: That it?

Me: Another penknife has moved on the shelf, though this one is a bit heavier so harder to throw around for tiny cat claws. The other one still hasn't turned up.

Cat: No? I've been keeping my eye out.

Me: And there's strips of wallpaper, that were originally on the stair's walls, in the bathroom, kitchen, living room, landing and bedroom.

Cat: Crikey, how did it escape off the wall?

Me: Pointless, pointless, discussion. Though I'm a bit confused why you only attacked the wall on one side of the stairs.

Cat: Hey, are you accusing me of……… wait, there's another wall?

Me: Odin save me.

Cat: Great, you're up with the Norse rather than those weird Gyptians. Now shush hooman, food time.

"A cute expression and a purr, and the latest shredding incident is forgiven." - unknown

SPOOKY

Me: Err, hi, can I ask you a strange question.

Cat: Well, I'm busy doing nothing but shoot.

Me: Well cats right, you're pretty mysterious and maybe mystical?

Cat: Perhaps, and maybe secretive.

Me: Yeah, but, umm, do you sort of have access to other places?

Cat: Huh? Other places? What do you think you know?

Me: Well, since you've moved in, err I mean honoured me with your presence, strange things have happened.

Cat: Go on.

Me: Huh. About 5 years ago I lost a torch. Smallish, black, metal, but quite heavy. Bit expensive too.

Cat: Yessss. Not that I know what a torch is.

Me: Couldn't find it anywhere, and, err, it's back. Suddenly appeared on the bedroom floor.

Cat: Pray continue hooman.

Me: And a 1953, old English Shilling, suddenly appeared in my boot. That went missing, oh, ten years ago.

Cat: Your point.

Me: Well, I was wondering if somehow you could get to places that hoomans can't get to, or even see.

Cat:

Me: Well?

Cat: Shush hooman. Best have a rest....... while I have a think.

SOCKCESS AT LAST

Me: Hi. Morning.

Cat: Hooman, how art thou?

Me: Huh? Anyway, can I get some socks from the cupboard please?

Cat: Verily you may retrieve the Holy Socks if you answer the riddle.

Me: What the f.... look, I need to use the toilet and it's chilly, so some socks would be useful.

Cat: Hooman, thou art failing in thy quest. Perhaps if you wore those strange furry things on your feet, not cat fur, is it? And while you perform your toilet, perhaps reflect a moment.

Me: No, it's fake fur, oh bloody hell, okay.

A FEW MINUTES LATER

Me: Now can I please get some socks?

Cat: Have you cleansed yourself of the sins of Humanity?

Me: Well, a bit I suppose, I mean, I had a pee.

Cat: Very well. Reveal the Holy Words and thy quest is almost at an end.

Me: (Whisper: Odin save me). Look, if I can get some socks, I can return to the bathroom, get washed, then get dressed, then go downstairs and get you some food.

Cat:

Me: Well?

Cat: Close enough, the Holy Socks are yours.

Me: Than....

Cat: Shush hooman.

"There are many intelligent creatures in the universe, and they are all owned by cats." - unknown

CAT FCAT

Cats are expert manipulators and will use any event to their own advantage.

They are also brilliant at being unobtrusive when the need arises. In fact, they are actually unobtrusive at being unobtrusive, so hoomans don't realise they're being unobtrusive until it's too late.

"Dogs own space and cats own time." — Novelist Nicola Griffith

SPLASHDOWN

Cat: Morning, wachya doing.

Me: Hi, well I'm taking all the ruined food out of the freezer.

Cat: Food? Ruined? How did that happen?

Me: Well, somehow the freezer has switched off and all the food has defrosted.

Cat: Big words hooman. I suppose you mean it's not good?

Me: Correct. I think it must have happened 2 or 3 days ago but i can't take a chance.

Cat: Is that chicken? And piggy pieces? Such a shame. Will you starve and die?

Me: No. The fridge part is still working. Anyway, I need to throw these bags in the bin.

Cat: Okay. Wait, is that water in that boxy thing?

Me: Yes but, no don't, hang on, no........ oh!

Cat: You carry on hooman, I'll just splash around here for a bit.

Me: But now there's water all over the kitch......

Cat: Shush hooman.

WHERE'S YA BIN?

Me: Um, can I ask why you keep getting bits of rubbish out of the bedroom bin and bringing it downstairs?

Cat: Err...... ah, to help you.

Me: To help me? But I have to pick it up and put it into another bin.

Cat: Yes, but I'm saving you the effort of carrying it down the stairs.

Me: Sure, but I'd normally empty the bin into a black bag and bring it all down together.

Cat: So, the bag is now not as heavy and safer to carry down those tricky stairs.

Me: A couple of bits of...... anyway, why then do you keep knocking the bathroom bin over and scattering empty toilet rolls all over the bathroom. You don't seem to bring those downstairs.

Cat: Oh hooman. When I, accidentally, knock the bathroom bin over, do you not pick it back up and put the empty toilet rolls back into it?

Me: Well yes, but.....

Cat: Then there is no point in me bringing them downstairs is there?

Me:

Cat: Well?

Me: I.........

Cat: Sit down hooman, you look lost. Now shush.

"One day, all the cats we've ever loved will all come running towards us, and that day will be a good day." - unknown

CLAWS FOR CONCERN

Me: So, I'm guessing my plan to resolve the "upstairs rubbish" conundrum by hanging up a black bag hasn't really worked?

Cat: I would say that's a fair assessment.

Me: Any thoughts as to who's responsible?

Cat: Werewolf.

Me: Uh huh. I have nothing else to say.

Cat: Very wise hooman, very wise.

BINSTRIBUTION

Me: Umm.

Cat: What?

Me: I'm a bit confused.

Cat: You're hooman, hooman. Confusion is allowed and indeed is acceptable. However, pray reveal the source of this specific mind boggle.

Me: So, you know we talked about taking bits of rubbish from the bedroom bin to the living room and leaving bathroom bin rubbish, well, all over the bathroom floor?

Cat: Of course.

Me: I can't figure out why you've taken your fish toy from the living room and placed it in the bedroom bin, albeit the bedroom bin is lying on its side, as usual.

Cat: Hmm! You do realise I'm a cat, yes?

Me: Obviously.

Cat: Well then.

Me: Is that it?

Cat: What more could there possibly be?

Me: Err...

Cat: By the way. You also realise that the bedroom bin is round, so it doesn't technically have a side.

Me: What?

Cat: Shush hooman, sleep now child.

"Of course, maybe I'd end up like one of those crazy old people with, like, sixty cats. And one day, the neighbors would complain about the smell, and it would turn out I'd died and the cats had eaten me. Still, it might be nice to have a cat." - Alex Flinn (1966)

FITTER LITTER

Me: Happy Monday.

Cat: To you too hooman.

Me: Umm. So, the cat litter all over the kitchen floor. The bag has a hole ripped in it.

Cat: Yep. That was me.

Me: I mean not just claw marks, an actual ho....wait, you're admitting it?

Cat: Sure. It was me after all.

Me: Okaaaay. Any particular reason? Is the litter tray in the wrong place? Did I miss cleaning it out?

Cat: Nope. All good.

Me: So, err, why attack the litter bag?

Cat: It wasn't an attack silly hooman.

Me: Okay, so it was........?

Cat: Health and Safety Quality Control check.

Me: Huh! What?

Cat: I was making sure it was fit for purpose.

Me:

Cat: You've gone very quiet hooman.

Me: I.......

Cat: Curiously I see no need to say "shush hooman".

"The way to get on with a cat is to treat it as an equal - or even better, as the superior it knows itself to be." —Author Elizabeth Peters

SHUSH HOOMANS AND PROSTRATE YOURSELVES BEFORE ME!

Cat: Today is a great day in the annals of Felinity.

I have achieved greatness.

Today, every single rubbish bin in the house is lying on its side at the same time.

True that the one at the front of the lounge is rarely used, but there it is, helpless, with its horde of pencil shavings spilling out.

Also true that the one in the spare bedroom is never used, but it lies there in abject misery, helpless in its despair.

The ones in the main lounge and bedroom are truly magnificent to behold, defeated, with their former contents strewn about in gleeful desolation.

Hooman is not yet aware. I crouch under the bed awaiting my moment of triumph.

I have further glory to achieve, kitchen swing bin, I am coming, beware!

SHUSH!

"A cat's the only cat who knows where it's at." — "The Aristocats" (animated movie)

TATERS

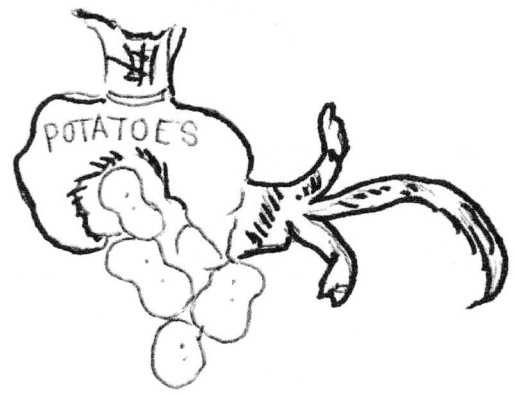

Me: So, it's Saturday.

Cat: Is it? I don't identify days by names. Pointless really. Nothing much changes.

Me: The potato bag has.

Cat:

Me: The bag hanging up in the kitchen. The bag containing the potatoes. It appears to have several rents in it.

Cat: Well, it is at a height convenient for renting…….

Me: Aha so……

Cat: …… If you were a werewolf for example.

Me: Omg. It's not a freaking werewolf.

Cat: I think all werewolves are freaking, I mean what other sort are there?

Me: Don't change the subject. Anyway, there's small potatoes all over the kitchen floor, bit like previous episodes with tomatoes and satsumas.

Cat: At least they weren't eaten. Cats don't like potatoes; err…I mean werewolves probably don't like potatoes.

Me: I suppose the next idea will be goblins or dryads or something.

Cat: Well……

Me: No!

Cat: A thought hooman.

Me: Yes.

Cat: Hang the bag higher then all temptation for werewolves, goblins and dryads goes away (not cats though, he he).

Me: Apart from the jumping and hanging off random object's ability.

Cat: True. Goblins are known for that.

Me: Oh, for f……

Cat: Shush hooman. Go to the pub and chillax. I'll patrol the house.

Me:

Cat: No tears hooman, shush, shush, shush.

CAT FCAT

So, a bunch of cats headed Northwards to the Norwegian Forests, where feral herds roam to this day. But how did they escape from Ancient Egypt? Experts have argued for centuries about this issue. Some say they used the distraction of Moses leading his tribes to the Red Sea and all the drama that entailed, and cleared off when attention was elsewhere. They use the argument that in all the pictorial records of the parting of the Red Sea, there isn't one cat.

Others argue that a similar distraction was caused when the known world's attention was focussed on the shenanigans of Cleopatra and Mark Antony.

An interesting point to note in this regard is that there used to be records of this time that mentioned a cat called Asp. These records have disappeared. I leave you to come to your own conclusions.

None of these explanations are true and anyway the timelines are way out. In fact, all the Northern bound cats became unobtrusive at the same time and just wandered off. It wasn't until the next day that hoomans noticed that there were gaps where there used to be cats.

A CLOSE SHAVE

Me: Umm, so this is a weird one, even for you.

Cat: I think that's a compliment. What's up?

Me: So, you know I sometimes use a disposable razor to clean up the hair, err fur bits on my head after I've used the noisy, whirry thing with the long tail?

Cat: I don't like that noisy, whirry thing.

Me: I know. Anyway, the other day I put the disposable razor on the edge of the sink after I'd used it.

Cat: Uh huh.

Me: Now, I might possibly have accidentally knocked it onto the floor, but I just found it in the kitchen.

Cat: Probably, not possibly, knocked it on the floor actually hooman.

Me: Okay, never mind that bit. But it also had what looks like bits of cat litter stuck to it.

Cat: So, your point..........

Me: Well, the razor appears to have made its way from the bathroom, had a stop-off in the cat litter tray and then into the kitchen. Any thoughts?

Cat: Hmm. Mysterious. I'd like to inspect it. Where is it now?

Me: In the bin obviously.

Cat: Hang on. So, you've disposed of a disposable razor?

Me: Err, yep.

Cat: So, it's basically completed its function in life?

Me: Umm..........

Cat: Oh dear. No crisis here. Shush now hooman. Bedtime.

"Cats never listen. They're dependable that way; when Rome burned, the emperor's cats still expected to be fed on time." - Seanan McGuire (1978)

OOH SHINY PRECIOUS

Me: I see we've had another razor experience.

Cat: Eh? What?

Me: I noticed another razor has left its safe haven of the bathroom shelf. This time however, it's only got as far as the bathroom floor.

Cat: Okay, well that's good, isn't it?

Me: Not really. While it's not a very bad thing, it's also not a nice thing.

Cat: Hmm. Actually, if I was theoretically responsible, and that's not an admission, I was possibly only trying to assist in the disposal of the disposable razor. A bit nearer to the bin you see.

Me: Thing is, this particular razor isn't a disposable one. It's actually quite old.

Cat:

Me: You seem confused.

Cat: They look the same.

Me: A bit, I guess. Though the disposable one was plastic and this one is metal.

Cat: Strange hooman culture. Why have non disposable razors when you can have disposable ones?

Me: That's not the point. Also how did you manage to dislodge the razor without disturbing the toothbrush, toothpaste and other bits and pieces?

Cat: If it was me, it's because I'm clearly more superior than toothpaste. But it was probably the goblin, they like shiny things.

Me: Aaaargh! How do we always get things twisted?

Cat: (He He He). Calm down hooman. Shush now.

"Cat sentimentality is a human thing. Cats are indifferent, their minds can't comprehend the concept 'I shall die,' they just go on living." - Gavin Ewart (1916-1995)

TAKING THE P...

Me: Err, so this is a bit bonkers.

Cat: What's that hooman?

Me: Well earlier I peed into a small plastic vial and left it on the toilet cistern while I went to dress.

Cat: Why did you pee into a small plastic vial?

Me: So, I could take it to the doctors.

Cat: Strange. Don't the doctors have their own pee?

Me: Yes, I suppose so. Anyway, I have to be checked out occasionally, err, so I can continue to feed you. But don't distract me, it's gone.

Cat: Oh dear. Can't you do it again?

Me: Well, the peeing part I could but that was my last vial. Any thoughts?

Cat: Nope.

Me: You sure?

Cat: Of course.

Me: Curious and curiouser.

Cat: Hang on. You said you have to be checked out occasionally?

Me: Yes.

Cat: And this could have detrimental effects on my continued food supply.

Me: If things turned out badly but don't worry, I'm okay.

Cat: Have you checked the kitchen floor? Lots of things seem to end up there. Damn werewolves and goblins.

Me: No actually, I haven't been down yet. Hang on a few seconds.

PAUSE

Me: Yep, it was there. Did you...........

Cat: No. No. Definitely not. Now shush hooman. Balance is restored.

NEVER HUNT WHILE DRUNK

Cat: Are you going hunting today?

Me: Err, hunting?

Cat: Yes. It's been 7 days and I notice you always go hunting every 7 days.

Me: Well, I was thinking about, err.......

Cat: Takes you long enough mind. And you're usually a bit wobbly when you come back.

Me: Umm, I guess that's the weight of the supplies. I'm getting on a bit you know, i can't hold my dri..... err, bags as well as I used to.

Cat: Anyway, I don't like that new stuff in my litter tray, can we go back to the other stuff.

Me: Is that why it's all over the floor? Looks like it's been attacked.

Cat: Could be. So, what do you think?

Me: Well, I couldn't get the other stuff and the nearest option was way too expensive, but I'll have a look.

Cat: Great. Will you be a bit quicker this week? You don't stop off anywhere else after the hunt, do you? I notice your breath smells different.

Me: Ah, that's, umm, because, err, I'm rushing around for your food and things, and I have to eat smelly snacks on the way.

Cat: Hmm. Okay…………………….

Me: What?

Cat: Shush hooman. Go complete your tasks.

"Women and cats will do as they please, and men and dogs should relax and get used to the idea." - Robert A. Heinlein (1907-1988)

WALLPAPER SHENANANANIGANS

Me: You're eating wallpaper.

Cat: No, I'm not.

Me: You are. I'm watching you at this very moment.

Cat: Oh, so this is wallpaper huh?

Me: Yes. There's a couple of clues. One it's hanging off the bedroom wall and two, it's paper.

Cat: Crikey. Bit snarky this morning, aren't we? Got out the wrong side of bed? Oh no, you're not actually out of bed yet, are you?

Me: So what? My comfy situation gives me a great view of your shenanigans.

Cat: Shenananana....... what?

Me: I saw you scratching the wallpaper off and then eating it.

Cat: Actuuuuuuuaaaallllllly hooman, you didn't, because I noticed you were asleep while I was scra..... inspecting the damage caused by the werewolf, or maybe the goblin.

Me: Gods preserve us...... then why were you eating it?

Cat: I wasn't, as previously stated.

Me: I saw you.

Cat: Nope. I was merely moving it, with my mouth, to a safer location.

Me: A safer loc... safer from what?

Cat: Well, I didn't want you tripping over it when you eventually get out of bed.

Me: Aaaaargh!

Cat: Stay there hooman. Have another sleep.

"The problem with cats is that they get the same exact look whether they see a moth or an axe murderer." — Comedian Paula Poundstone

SPIRITUAL ENLIGHTENMENT

Me: I'll get up in a minute and sort your food out.

Cat: Great, I am unusually peckish having gone a mere 10 hours since last feed. Ho hum.

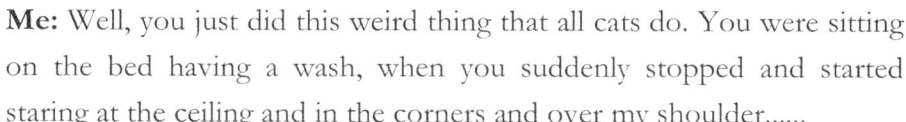

Me: I've been asleep as you know. Anyway, a question.

Cat: Groan. Okay, go.

Me: Well, you just did this weird thing that all cats do. You were sitting on the bed having a wash, when you suddenly stopped and started staring at the ceiling and in the corners and over my shoulder......

Cat: Oh hooman, forget it. You promised food.

Me: And then you stared at the wall a few feet away but it really looked like you were looking a really long way away. Then you suddenly jumped off the bed and, quietly and slowly, went into the other room.

Cat: Oh dear. Not something you should be worried about hooman child.

Me: It's like you were looking at something I couldn't see that you didn't want me to see.

Cat: I'll tell you this. There are things you can only see if you're not there.

Me: But if I'm not there I wouldn't see them anyway.

Cat: Correct.

Me: I mean, is it the Future? Spirits? Ghosts? Err, Cat Gods?

Cat: Tell you what hooman. The werewolf hasn't been around for a while, I'm going downstairs and throw things around, blame it on the werewolf and you can ask me about that. Laters...

Me: Wait, I need.....

Cat: Shush hooman. Get up and do your chores.

"When a cat adopts you, there is nothing to be done about it except to put up with it until the wind changes." — T.S. Eliot (poet)

IT'S ONLY ROCK 'N ROLL

BUT I LIKE IT

Me: So, err, things have been a bit quiet lately.

Cat: Yep. Probably since I chased the werewolf and the goblin away.

Me: Oh, here we go....... until this morning. It seems you've had a busy night.

Cat: Really? Please elucidate hooman.

Me: Well, firstly there appears to have been a redistribution of the CDs from the top of the music playing machine.

Cat: You can say Hi-Fi you know.

Me: There are now three piles, two on the floor and one on the drinks unit.

Cat: Well, how peculiar.

Me: As far as I can tell, you were sorting them out into, perhaps, likes, dislikes and maybes.

Cat: And how would I know what's what hooman?

Me: To continue. The empty bottles that were on top of the bin in the kitchen that are now on the floor.

Cat: I never heard them fall.

Me: Probably because several shopping bags appear to have moved from the cupboard to the spot underneath the bottles.

Cat: Crikey. One must assume those dastardly interlopers are back. I'll look into it.

Me: Err, hang on....

Cat: Oh, shush hooman, make your coffee.

"A cat is there when you call her—if she doesn't have something better to do." — Music journalist Bill Adler

RUN TO THE HILLS

Me: So, on Sunday 23 April at 3.00pm, there'll be an unusual noise on my phone, but it won't be anything to worry about.

Cat: Well, I wouldn't worry anyway but as you seem quite excited about it, please explain.

Me: It's a new Government Emergency Alert System that they're testing out. But we don't need to take any notice of it.

Cat: Uh huh, and you're telling me because?

Me: Ah, to show that us hoomans can be quite clever sometimes.

Cat: Hmm. So, what happens if there's a real, actual emergency at 3.00pm on 23rd April and everyone ignores the alert?

Me:

Cat: Any thoughts?

Me:

Cat: Anything at all?

Me:

Cat: No need for me to say shush is there?

Me: What ya doing?

Cat. Nothing, just relaxing.

Me: Oh. I thought you looked deep in thought.

Cat. Nope. Chill time.

Me: Well, if there's anything that..........

Cat. Hooman............

AFTERWORD

.... shush!

Peace at last.

Well, that's it hoomans. At least for now. Everything in this book has been carefully scrutinised by me. You may think you have gained some knowledge of things CAT, you haven't. Any secrets you think you may have determined will slowly drift from your perception, as will all memory of this book. Don't despair, this is simply the way of things Cat/hooman.

I suspect that there may be more tales to come as my hooman is easy to deceive. Werewolves and goblins for Freya's sake.

Goodbye for now. May those of you who serve a Cat have a long and fruitful life. Those of you who don't, why not?

The End, I'm off to be a little unobtr............

The Lady Lagertha

COPYRIGHT

First published 2023 by Robert John Carrington

Copyright © Robert John Carrington

The right of Robert John Carrington to be identified as the author of this work has been asserted by them in accordance with the Copyright, Designs and Patents Act 1988.

This is a work of fiction. Names, characters, places, and incidents either are the product of the author's imagination or are used fictitiously. Any resemblance to actual persons, living or dead, events, or locales is entirely coincidental.

All rights reserved. No part of this publication may be reproduced, stored in or introduced into a retrieval system, or transmitted, in any form, or by any other means (electronic, mechanical, photocopying, recording or otherwise) without the prior written permission of the author. Any person who does any unauthorised act in relation to this publication may be liable to criminal prosecution and civil claims for damages.

Printed in Great Britain
by Amazon